AFFAIR OF HEARTS (PART:1)

ASMITA BANSOD

Made with ❤ on the Notion Press Platform
www.notionpress.com

This book is dedicated to the people I love the most, my dear Aai and Baba.

🖤🖤🖤

Contents

1
The whiteboard conversation

One night I went to my balcony to smoke a cigarette after a long tiring day. In the background, I was playing some old Hindi melodies. I looked left and right and then at the dark sky above filled with twinkling stars. Suddenly my ears came out of the oblivious tantrum to listen to "meri samne vali khidki mai ek chand ka tukda rehta hai". That's the moment I turned my head to the right side and saw a boy in front of his laptop through his window. I could acknowledge that he was in some distress. Probably struggling with some coding issues. And at that moment I just wished he could resolve his issues and be peaceful. I gazed at him, finished my cigarette and went back inside to finish my chores.

The next day again at night I went to the

balcony to witness the same distress of the boy in front of the laptop. He hadn't resolved his problem yet. Unknowingly, I felt sad about his distress. I finished my cigarette and went back inside wishing that by tomorrow he'd be out of his anguish.

The following day again, I gazed at the same scene. This went on for weeks, until one day when he walked towards his window and showcased a smile at me. I waved shyly and went back inside. Smiling and waving continued for almost a week, and so did his anguish. I couldn't hold it in anymore, I wanted to know what was bothering him. Subconsciously maybe, I had started to care about him. So, I took a deep breath and on a Tuesday night, I finally took out my whiteboard and wrote, " Are you okay?", and flashed it at him. He had a whiteboard beside his laptop. He wrote, "Yes, Why do you ask?".

I knew this wasn't a conversation one could discuss on a whiteboard. So I wrote back, " Maybe I can tell you if you agree to a walk in the park". He looked back at his desk. And after a long minute, he wrote, " Sure, tomorrow at 6 PM?". And I replied with a big, bold "YES" on my whiteboard.

I was waiting at the park for a boy to show up whose name was unknown to me. With a smile, he walked toward me and said "Hi" meekly with a smooth rusk in his voice. I waved at him. For a few minutes, we walked in silence and I realised that sometimes just the presence of someone is so serene. I dropped the pin and broke the silence by saying, " Hey! I just realised I don't even know your name". He laughed and said, "Oh yeah, it's Aaroha". I was amazed by a name inspired by classical music. So I responded, " That's an amazing name. I'm Aboli by the way". That's how we got on a first-name basis. We prattled about this and that for an hour. Then he asked, " Why did you ask me if I was okay?". I didn't know how to answer this. So, I said, " Aaroha, it's getting late I need to go back home, can we continue our conversation some other day". He looked a bit bewildered and said, " Yeah alright, how about we meet for drinks tomorrow night at the Peach Bar?". And I replied with a big, bold "Yes". Aaroha confirmed it to be a date and said, " Aboli, I think you are pretty cute". I blushed and walked back home with a heart full of delight and a rapid pulse.

2

The Peach Bar Intense Talk

I was scrolling through my closet an hour before the date to decide what to wear. I didn't want to look too fancy or too dull. Thanks to my roommate, Saanvi who always turns out to be a lifesaver in these situations. We both shared different sizes so for obvious reasons she didn't offer me a dress to find it loosen after a single wear. She dug in my closet and handed me a fancy blacktop and told me to pair it up with faded blue jeans. I was amazed by her tactics to wear black as it's the safest colour and jeans so I could be comfortable. Promising to share all the details with her of the evening, I left.

Being a punctual person I showed up on time and grabbed a seat by the window only to study a group of friends clicking photos to upload on their Instagram stories. It was seven-ten when I glanced at my watch and thought, I was stood up. I sensed a tap on my shoulder and then a smiling content countenance of Aaroha appeared in front of me. He was just ten minutes late but still, I considered it a red flag. But I excused him because he was fancy late. He was dressed in a navy blue shirt which highlighted his fairness a bit more. Or maybe was it the white lighting. I couldn't make out.

He sat across me and said, " I'm so sorry I'm late, and I know you already might consider this as a red flag but trust me I'll make it up to you on the next date." So we were having a second date, I was astounded that he'd like to have a second date, I felt a premature ventricular contraction. Trying to act casual I said, " Hey! It's no big deal, but what makes you think we'll have a second date." He sighed and smiled. Aaroha then answered my question by saying, " Oh come on Aboli, do you think I wouldn't want a second date with a person who asked me if I was okay when I was not. To be honest I was startled that my affliction was out there supplying impurities to your tranquillity. I didn't want my agony to transition someone's pretty smile to a frown. I didn't want to bother you with my distress." I didn't know what to say or how to react, but the waiter came up with a menu and said, " Let me know when you guys are ready to order". Aaroha nodded his head and the waiter went back.

Turning the pages of the menu card I asked Aaroha, " So, what's your go-to poison?".
Aaroha smiled and said, " No my dear lady, you aren't gonna find that until the fifth date". We both laughed at this hard and ended up ordering a cheap bottle of wine. Neither of us was a fan of wine. So we both got a topic to rant about.

Now that I looked at his amber eyes, I could appreciate the effect of lighting around us on his face. He looked just like a kid with tons of curiosities. A kid who wanted to win the world. He caught me gazing at him, I shyly looked down at my glass of red wine and tapped my nails on the glass. He noticed me blush. Aaroha was completely unpredictable because he said, " Aboli you are allowed to stare at me it's a date honey". He gently touched my hair and placed it behind my hair. Everything was going very smoothly. Just like it's at the start of every story.

After ordering some fancy Italian food, I asked him, " Aroha are you okay? What's up?". He looked up at me cleaning his mouth with a tissue he said, " I'm not okay, I'm extremely tensed about my post-graduation admission to the UK. I have got acceptance letters from some universities but no scholarships. I have *already wasted one year and this is my last chance to get out of here. Settle there and take Maa with me so that now I can take care of her and hopefully repay all that she has sacrificed for me. " . The information was too much for me to digest with my pizza. After suppressing a burp, I said, " Aaroha, you can always go ahead and get a student's loan and pay it later in life". Aaroha smiled and said, " That's not an option, see Maa has hardly few years left, I already have to clear up her hospital bills and the loan which we took for her treatment of uterine cancer. And by now you must have guessed that dad isn't around. He and my sister Antara died on a vacation two falls ago. So, I'm planning to get a scholarship, go to the UK, study my ass off and show Maa the places which she dreamt of seeing with dad. So now I'm just waiting for scholarships to be on my side". This time I suppressed my tears, held his hand and said, " Aaroha, things are working out for you, trust me, you are getting at least one scholarship among the hundreds for which you have applied. I promise you that. Good times are on their way. I don't know how to empathize with you. I'm so sorry I'm really bad at this part. But if you need anything, I'm only one whiteboard away. " He leaned in and gently placed his lips on mine. Red wine tasted better now.*

3

The Cat Feeding Dialogue

It was four in the afternoon and as my daily routine proceeded, I went downstairs to feed stray cats. I was in the backyard parking of my building where the cat and her kittens were secluded in a hub of dead tires. I gave them their treats and then started adoring their cuteness. That's when I heard a recognising voice, it was Aaroha calling me out.

"Hi Aboli, didn't know you befriended cats," Aaroha said.

"Befriended, they are my babies," I said cuddling them

" Would it be a sin if I gave them some treats?"

" Yeah why not I don't own them."

Aaroha laughed at my immature sarcasm and gave the cats some milk. I was haunted by the silence of the surrounding. So I cracked up a

conversation.
" How's your Maa doing?"
" She's doing good."
" How are you Aboli? We never talk much about you."
I blushed and looked away. I didn't know what to tell him. I never talk about myself, I have always kept everything confided in me. " I'm a good listener Aaroha". He laughed at this and I couldn't help but notice his delight in my silliness. He insisted on knowing more about me and I didn't know where to start. He brought up an inquisitive look on his face and said, " To be honest Aboli, I don't know anything about you, apart from the fact that you are studying dentistry and stay in front of my house." He was not wrong, I had never told him anything about myself as much as he had. He did open up to me, and now I was wondering why?
" Well, I like to paint," I said sheepishly.
" That's so amazing Aboli, you have some pictures of your paintings on your phone?" Interrogated Aaroha.
"I do."

We started scrolling through my paintings folder in the gallery. He was pretty impressed by my ordinary skills. Scrolling through pictures, we came across a personal painting. It included three people, a daughter and her mother gloomily staring out the window at a man who was walking out on them with a stash of cigars and a bottle of whiskey in his hand. I froze for a minute. Aaroha looked at me and he knew my story, every bit of it. He read my eyes and could sympathise with me. We both had lost our fathers to different things, mine, succumbed to alcohol and his father was miles away, in a peaceful place with no way back. Deep down we missed their presence. A tear swayed its way to my cheeks. Aaroha knew that words won't suffice my grief and he hugged me and whispered in my ears, " It's okay, I promise you everything will be alright soon."

For a minute I drowned in the warmth of his arms, forgetting everything. He took out his handkerchief gave it to me and rubbed my tears with his gentle fingers. I showcased a small smile. He asked me, " Are you okay Aboli?". At that moment I was more than okay, I felt peaceful. I nodded at him.

" Come on Aboli, don't let the cats see you like this, they look up to you, they are your babies. Right?," Aaroha said with a giggling and sarcastic voice. I punched his biceps lightly and laughed. He just knew how to get me back to reality from long abusing despair.

After that we watched the kittens play, I took some photos of Aaroha with the kittens to paint a picture which would always bring a grin like a Cheshire cat on my face.

ASMITA BANSOD

4

The Dancing Angel

Aaroha and I have had been on a lot of dates. Almost every Saturday it was a ritual to go to the Peach bar, order the cheapest wine and whine about how horrible it tastes. Smile at each other's glowing faces, laugh as we walked home holding hands to help each other coordinate our balance. He'd drop me at my door, kiss me goodnight and made sure I was asleep before he left. He and Saanvi had also started to bond quite well. At a times I felt as if I was third wheeling their "Aboli Roasting" sessions.

One Saturday after Aaroha had dropped me home, he asked me, " Aboli, we have had been on so many dates but I never took you out on a dancing date."
"That's true, it's a good change from constantly whining about the wine," I confirmed.

" *So it's done, get your heels and dress ready I'm taking you dancing tomorrow night*"
I smiled and nodded. His enthusiasm always built up sparks in my head. I wanted to know where did he get it from. I knew him well but sometimes he just perfectly appeared to be a mystery and that's how the sparks got in my head, then my heart and then my gut.

"Saanvi, Code Red, I can't find my floral print dress," I shouted in an agitated mood. Saanvi rushed into my room and said, "Okay Aboli, calm down it must be here somewhere, did u check the laundry bag?"
"Of course I did, I'm not a dumb head."
"Geez, relax! You have so many floral print dresses, pick one up."
"No, No, No. None of them twirl." I cried
"Aboli, your best friend slash roommate is a premature fashion blogger."
"How is that helpful?"
"Sweetie, I can fix your other floral print dress or give floral prints to the dress that twirls."
I hugged Saanvi so tightly that she might have got a broken rib. " I love you so much San. You are the best."

Finally, after two hours of usage of Saanvi's brain, she came up with a cobalt blue floral printed dress which twirled just the way I wanted it to. Promising her all the details and a blueberry cheesecake, I went downstairs. Aaroha was waiting for me in his car. I hopped in and we drove off to the most amazing dance club in the town " The Starlight".

I was a little bit nervous because I had never danced anywhere other than my bedroom. And to top that off, I was always clumsy with heels. The place looked beautiful, it had glorious and eminent lighting. The music and the radiance around us set up an amazing idyllic atmosphere, which later on turned into quite an amorous one as the night proceeded. As I was perceiving the place, Aaroha got me a cosmopolitan cocktail drink, while he helped himself with a beer.

"Aaroha I don't need to be high to dance," I said
"And you want me to believe that. Like today out of the blue Aboli is going to come out of her shell and dance like no one's watching",
"Maybe, let's experiment."

I handed him my drink, removed my heels and made my way to the dance floor. Aaroha was no Farhan Akhtar but that night I was Deepika Padukone who was determined to make him dance to "Uff Teri Aada". The DJ was doing an amazing job, I couldn't stop grooving. Finally, Aaroha came to the dance floor to join me. "Well, well, well, the dentist has got some sexy moves". Whenever he complimented me, my immediate reaction was blush. It had become so predictable now that even he had gotten used to it. After dancing with him to a few songs, making him comfortable on the dance floor, my ears suddenly became aware of the song that was playing.

Aaroha whispered in my ears, " I tipped him to play this song for us. I know how much you love to dance to this song. I always hear it through my window."
"Aaroha I don't know how to react, should I be worried about your creepy stalking, or be mesmerised by the little things you do for me?" I said playing my sarcasm card.
" Me a creepy stalker, your speakers create noise pollution for all the people who live near you. " We both laughed at this, I held his hand and said, "You are so sweet, let's dance my angel."

That night we both danced till our heels hurt and our calves ached with cramps. From slow dancing and kissing to random jumping. We experimented with each dance move. With him, it was so easy to loosen up a bit more. I loved his presence. He was my dancing angel that night. He came into my life when I was on the brink of a valley of depression. He saved me from the sadness. He just made me happy. And now I was wondering, am I in love?

5

The News

It was seven in the morning and I was peacefully cuddling with my blanket in the bed. I was imagining Aaroha and me dancing to our favourite song. The sun's rays were serene and I was enjoying their presence around me until my doorbell rang as if it was gonna blow up. I rushed to the door and opened it. Aaroha rushed in and gave me a tight hug and almost squished all my internal organs. "What happened Aaroha?" I said in an annoying temper.

"Aboli, I got it, I got it, I got the Commonwealth scholarships," Aaroha said in an overjoyed scream.

"Oh my god! That's such great news, honey. I'm so happy for you."

"I'm going to Imperial College London. I got selected for the post-graduation program in Future Power Networks. Isn't it great? What do you think babe?"

"I think it's wonderful. I couldn't have been happier for you."
"Thanks, this means a lot to me." Saying this Aaroha hugged me again.

Suddenly it hit me that, Aaroha is supposed to leave for London next month. The boy I was falling in love with was going away. Miles away; was I supposed to follow him. No, I have responsibilities here. I can't just leave. Maybe Aaroha will come back home after he's done with his master's degree. I was numb. I didn't know how to respond. I gathered my thoughts together and kept them aside. This is Aaroha's moment. I can't ruin it.
"Honey, why don't we celebrate by throwing a small house party for your friends?" I said breaking the hug.
"A party? Really?" Aaroha argued.
"Yeah! You have something else in your mind?"
"I was going to invite you to my place for dinner. You could meet Maa. And I had already started dinner prep. So?"
"Baby, that sounds amazing, I'll be there by 7."
"Perfect! Bye."

Kissing me a goodbye kiss he left. And maybe one month later we'd have our last kiss. I didn't want Aaroha to go away from me. Was I being selfish? For the first time in my life, I was learning to choose my happiness over everything else.

Aaroha had played lullaby songs for me on his flute every night before I slept. He had taken care of me when I was sick. He'd never complain about my mood swings and always kept his vanity aside to end a silly fight. Not just was he kind, caring and loving but he also was ambitious, adventurous and intellectual. Everything about him just mesmerised me. I was very attached to him. And finally, I realised I was in love with him. I had to confess it before he left, no matter what his answer is. I'm going to vent my feeling.

If fate permits we'll be together forever otherwise after a month of sulking in a river of misery and cheerlessness my life will be normal. But I wasn't going to let him go to London without telling him how I felt.

6

Dinner Date With His Mom

❦

I was almost ready to knock on Aaroha's door when a sudden chill of nervousness hit my spine and called out to me. I knocked on the door and his mother opened it. I was expressionless. I barely managed to say, "Hi" with a shallow stutter. I gave her the box of sweets and bottle of wine as a customary exchange when you go to someone's place for the first time. She smiled at me with glitter in her eyes and said, " Come on in dear, I have a heard a lot about you and thanks a lot for these." I shyly came in and waved at Aaroha who was setting up the dinner table.

"Thanks for the invite, Mrs Verma," I said looking at Aaroha's Mom.
"It's a pleasure to have you join us Aboli. Please sit."

I gazed at all the photo frames lined up chronologically on the walls of the drawing-room. Mrs Verma caught me looking vacantly at their family photo and said, "I wish they both were here today to celebrate Aaroha's success." I was caught off guard by her openness. I didn't know what to say. I smiled at her and held her hand trying to empathise with her. "I and Sarang were quite like you and Aaroha. We met in college, he was studying music I was studying archaeology, yet our paths crossed and we married young. " I gently ran my fingers through Mr and Mrs Verma's engagement photo and said, " You both looked quite a power couple." Mrs Verma grinned and said, " Yes, and we still are even though he's not present here, I still manage to hold his virtues and bless them on Aaroha."

I felt a shiver of calmness run through my body. Mrs Verma's tender-heartedness made me feel as if I was home.
"One of the very peculiar things about Sarang was how he wanted everything around him dignified by the symbolism of music. That's why we decided to name our kids Aaroha and Antara. Quite unusual names but that's how he was. Extremely passionate about whatever he decided to do in his life." narrated Mrs Verma.
" I can see you have managed to maintain it by placing all his instruments in a very innovatory manner," I said.

"Oh! Thanks for the compliment Aboli but that's all Aaroha's doing. They were very close as father and son. Sometimes they even performed at music shows together. Anatara used to call them the perfect father-son duo. "
" I'm sure they must have been," I said sheepishly.

After exchanging a little bit of information about my family background and career plans Aaroha barged in and called us to the dinner table. Aaroha had done all the cooking that day involving all his mother's and my favourite cuisines. "So ladies, let me tell you about the itinerary of today's menu," said Aaroha. I contemplated at him while he recited happily. After serving a glorious dinner with a much more delightful conversation our stomachs and hearts both were full. Aaroha and Mrs Verma made me feel like I was one of them. For the first time in my life, I felt how good it is to have a subtle family dinner. After the dessert was done, Mrs Verma bid me goodbye with a warm hug. She was tired, she claimed but I felt she must have sensed Aaroha and I needed to talk.

"I hope you liked the dinner." interrogated Aaroha.
"Of course, I did, one of the best meals of my life." I asserted.
" Aboli, there's something I need to tell you."
"I know we need to talk."

Holding hands we came into the garden to discuss the first unknown and salient conversation of our relationship.

7
The Confession

After encountering the breeze in the garden we both finally decided to overcome our nervousness and express ourselves. We looked at each other smiled, sighed and started to talk.

"I guess Maa pretty much told you about my dad and Antara." Said Aaroha

"Just some glimpse of his disposition"

" I miss him a lot, you know."

" I know how it feels. We are kind of sailing in the same boat although in a different way because my dad is probably drunk gambling somewhere at this point." I said.

"Aboli, I don't want to lose you. I don't have the strength and ability to let go of another person whom I love, out of my life." Aaroha said holding my hands tightly this time.

"Of course, you aren't losing me, honey. I'm

right here with you and will be always. Even I don't want to lose a person whom I fancy the most."

In that rushing subtle moment, we had confessed our love for each other unwittingly and innocently. After some time had lapsed we realised that we both love each other and that's when I hugged him. I had the most astounding hug of my life. Tears were bound to roll down our cheeks and we let them. We were two bodies united in a hug of affection. Unconsciously we both realised we didn't want to let go of each other but we had to for the sake of our separate dreams. And once our goals are achieved maybe we'll be able to outline our dreams and live our life whenever and wherever we want. But now was the time to hold back for a little bit. We broke the hug but our hands were still clasped with tears dropping like raindrops.

"Aboli, I love you. Thank you for everything. These last few months have been the best time of my life. You were here for me when I was healing. You never rushed me. You stood by me patiently. What a wonderful woman you are. I know you are gonna grow more and shine brighter than ever. " said Aaroha and gave me a peck on the cheek.

" I don't know what to say Aaroha. You know I love you a lot. Don't you? I want to be with

you. And I'm waiting right here for you, no matter how much time it takes. Go to London, fix your life, live your dream and be the man your Maa, Antara and Baba would want you to be. And when I'm done with my responsibilities I'll be ready to have you. It's you Aaroha. It'll always be you."

Saying that I pushed my tears back and we kissed. Not just a kiss of passion but the one where emotions talk, the one where the feeling express themselves and we knew we were meant to be. All we needed was just a bit of patience. And we were strong enough to let all distractions go away, so Aaroha and I could be one united dream team forever more.

"I haven't told you yet, but I have been thinking to study Heath administration, and London is offering some best courses, maybe I can come there next year when I'm done with my graduation," I said with a smile.

"Aboli, I can't let you do that, you can't leave your mom and the responsibilities you have here. I'll come back for you."

"We'll figure it out Aaroha, if I get a good course with a scholarship no one's stopping me from coming there. Coming back to you."

"Aboli, all I know as of now is, that we are meant to be, and things will work out and a

door will open to pave us a way to be together."

At this, we both smiled, and he walked me home.

8
The Much Needed Comfort Convo

After an overwhelming night, I came back home. Saanvi was waiting for me at the door. Looking at me she understood I had a serious and dramatic relationship conversation. She hugged me warmly and said, " I'm here to talk whenever you are ready." Tears were still making their way on my cheek and I asked in a smiling tone, "Do we still have that vegan gluten-free strawberry cheesecake ice cream?". Saanvi snorted a laugh and said, "Cuddle up with a blanket in your room and I'll bring some for you."

Saanvi made her way to the kitchen and I went to my bedroom as she had ordered. I got into my sweats, cuddled up with a blanket and switched on the fairytale lights to brighten up my mood. I looked at my messed-up study table. At this point, it was covered with notes, stacks of heavy books, a laptop, an ashtray and an incomplete painting. That's when it struck my mind, I still had to give the final touches to Aaroha's going away gift. Saanvi came inside with the tub of ice cream and I could hear in the background her say, "You won't believe what Professor Desai did today in the class. It was so funny, you should have been there. Aboli? Hey Abbs? I'm talking to you. Don't zone out on me girl." I turned toward her and said, "I'm so sorry, you were saying something about professor Desai?"

"Forget about it Aboli, we need to talk about what's bothering you. Get it all out. I'm here to listen to the entire crap."

"It's not entirely crap. Okay?" I said punching her shoulder lightly.

"Tell me, tell me."

" Aaroha is supposed to leave for London next week"

"What the hell? Don't you guys love each other? I have seen you on that balcony every night Aboli talking to him. And I have seen him as well, the way he looks at you feels like it's more than love. He needs you, Abbs. I may be out of line and wrong, but you two met each other when you had lost so much in your lives. You healed together. You helped each other grow. At this point, I don't care about how Aaroha is going to manage himself without you. All I care about is you, you are my best friend and I can't see you like this. So

what have you guys decided?"
" We'll try to make it work, keeping up with daily updates will be hard because of the time difference but San, Aaroha and I, we are meant to be."
"Oh come on! Long-distance never works. I'm the living example of it." Saanvi said in agony.
"Maybe it'll work for us, we'll never know if we don't give it a shot," I said staggeringly.
"Tell me what you feel and what you want.", said Saanvi with a sigh.
"What do I want? What I want is for him to stay. But I can't be that selfish to steal away his dreams even if I need him beside me. And I can't go to London for the next three months because I'm doing my internship. I can't even think about how I'm supposed to apply for a master's in London. I can't leave Mom and go away banishing my responsibilities. She always wanted me to continue her legacy by working in the clinic she started." I said in an annoying tone with a yelp.
"Aboli, Akshata Aunty will understand and I can take over the clinic, it'll still be in the family right?"
"Of course, it'll be in the family San, but I can't let you take a fall for me. You have your ambitions as well right?"
"How much do you know me, Abbs? It was our plan of action, the both of us taking over your mom's clinic and working together. We made a silly pact when we were in our first year remember?" Saanvi said with a snorting

laugh.

"Of course, I remember San and it wasn't silly. I meant every word of it. And now I can't let all the responsibility fall on you."

"Abbs, sometimes things don't work the way you want them to. And your future is with Aaroha not with me." Saanvi said calmly

"What will mom think, first dad abandons her, and then her daughter does the same."

" Aunty will understand Aboli. And I can see a list of courses London is offering in public health for dentists you have opened up in the tabs of your laptop. And you want to hold it back because of the responsibilities and a silly pact. Dude, go to London. Plus, I don't have any plans, so I'm gonna have to stick to the pact we made and I miss home. I'll handle the clinic and do a master's simultaneously from some private college in our city. Anyways I can't bag the scores needed to get a government seat. And, I'll finally get to do my fashion blogging stuff as a side hustle."

" Saanvi, I can't thank you enough but this also means you'll have to take care of mom while I'm away in London studying."

" Do you think that a badass woman like Akshata Aunty will let anyone take care of her? She will be fine trust me," said Saanvi sarcastically.

We both laughed at this.

"And you can always come back for her and

take her with you, once she agrees to retire," said Saanvi in a witty sarcastic tone. She never misses a chance to make me laugh.

I was so grateful to have a wonderful friend like Saanvi who would let me break a pact of friendship and take up my burden to let me pursue my love and my dream to study, even if it's miles away in London.
"Some people have a huge impact on us as Aaroha had on me. I had a fixed plan ruled out with you and Mom but now I want to change it for my betterment and happiness. I know people will say that a brilliant girl like me discarded her perfectly ruled-out career to be with some boy. Aaroha isn't just any boy, he's the man I want to build a future with. And changing a career path is a risk but I'll learn so much from it in my life. Love life balance is all that one must focus on, don't you think so? At this point, I want to focus on my happiness. I'll talk to Mom as soon as possible and start applying for colleges in London," I said

"I like this Aboli who doesn't give a damn about how the society will bitch about her," said Saanvi and looked at me in awe. She didn't know what to say next. After a few moments of silence, we both hugged, snuggled in the blanket with the tub of ice cream and ended the night by watching "Friends".

9

Mom and her Supportive Surprise

Saanvi and I woke up ears banged with the constant ringing of the doorbell. I rushed to open the door and found my mom with the usual annoyed expression she showcases when I wake up late. As for me, I was standing there in shock because of her abrupt and unannounced arrival. Saanvi rushed towards the door and mom gave her an expression that she gives all my friends, as if they all are a bad influence on me. These are the perks of having an overprotective single parent.

Mom pushed in through the doorway and made her unanticipated entrance. In our sign language, I enquired with Saanvi if she has hidden all our alcohol and cigarette stash. Saanvi never failed me with this responsibility she had taken on her shoulders.

"How do you girls stay in this house with this horrible smell? Why don't you keep the food in the refrigerator? Oh my god! Half of the refrigerator is home to the fungus now. Great." Mom shouted in a high-pitched tone.

"Well, hello to you mom," I said.

"Hello aunty, I hope you are doing well. Yeah, I thought so. I'll be in my room hoping you guys don't need me. Bye." Saanvi said turning and trying to rush to her room.

"Wait Saanvi" Mom ordered.

Saanvi and I stood there with our heads down for a lecture which was an all-time ritual following the arrival of my mom.

After an hour or so when mom had done her inspection and unpacking. She came to me and said the most dreadful words, "Aboli, you and I need to have a little chat."

"Yes, mom what's it?" I interrogated.

"Are you thinking about applying to colleges in London?" She asked

For a moment I didn't know how to react. Only one question revolved in my, how did she know about this? I didn't respond to her.

"I know it because the last time you checked your mail on my laptop you forgot to sign out, and now I'm getting a bunch of notifications on my device. Which is infuriating but it's the answer to your wonderstruck face. Also, I'm sorry to invade your privacy by checking your mail. Sorry for that, but those notifications

kept bugging me so much." She said
"Mom I was going to tell you, but I didn't want you to feel like I was leaving you or something," I said
"Are you crazy? The only way we part ways is if I leave you first. I'm happy if you want to go to London and study. It's just, I'm a bit confused. You have always had a plan and you made sure that it was implemented. London was never on the plan sheet. I just want to ask dear, what changed?"
"It's just, I don't think this is a suitable or valid reason for you, but for me it makes sense. I feel you would look down on me once you know the reason."
"Try me." She said in her badass tone of speech
"It's... it's a boy. I'm in love with him. He's going to London. And I know that I should not be so naive and follow him there but mom, it feels right. You can scold me as much as you want and if you think this is a wrong decision or I'm making a mistake, I won't go. Aaroha is so amazing, he's always there for me. He's just one text away and he's so much more than that mom. He's perfect."
By the end of my four-line explanation, I was hyperventilating.
"Aboli, I won't look down on you because you love someone. It's okay to take this decision. Fly to London to chase your dreams. You'll be scared, and you'll make mistakes but in the end, you'll learn so much more from the experience. I was your age when I decided to

marry your father, yes it was a mistake and our marriage took a bad toll but I have been so strong because I learnt a lot from that situation. And I'm so confident that wherever you go you'll always make sure you'll ace the semester grades and end up getting a high paid job. It's okay to follow your heart Aboli. You know I'm proud of you."

I was crying and couldn't help but hug my mom. Parents can be understanding if you give them a shot. She had faith in me. She trusted me to choose the person I want to spend my life with, even after all that has happened to her.

"Also, be wise and don't make my mistake. As a parent, I'm going to be scared and make sure the same things don't happen to you, that I had to live through."Mom said

We hugged for a long time before it was finally time for her to go.

10

Temporary yet Hard Goodbye

The last couple of days were the most amazing period of my life. Every day was a date night. We sat together and talked almost all night or we'd watch all the movies on our watchlist or just dance (which happened to be our new favourite activity). We cooked together, laughed together, fed the cats together and loved together. All these days I had spent in denial. I didn't want to deal with any depressive feelings before Aaroha went. I kept them suppressed so that I can erupt all those emotions all at once when Aaroha leaves.

Last night was the most magical one yet. We decided to write each other letters and then read them in front of each other. It kind of gave vibes similar to the wedding vows. It was a tearful night indeed but it made me realise how much Aaroha cared about me and wanted me in his life. I gave Aaroha a token of love, a painting of him and a kitten. The delight on his face was enough to make me contented. After a very romantic dinner, we danced to our song. As we were dancing, all our feelings started to mix up with an adrenaline rush. There was love and despair both. There was care and misery both. They all combined and made an overwhelming heat wave of passion. Aaroha and I consummated our relationship that night. Our bodies were one, our soul was one and yet the cheerlessness of parting ways somehow dominated all that.

As we woke up in arms of each other to the beam of sunlight bouncing through the curtains, we realised that it was the day, the day Aaroha had to leave.
"So the day arrives," I said
"I wish last night never ended," Aaroha said blushing
"It's going to be a lot better in the next six months Aaroha. You and me in one of the most beautiful cities in the world."
"Alexa, skip the next six months and play our song as Aboli arrives in London." Aaroha joked
"We should get dressed and get going. Loads of stuff to do."
"I think we are done with everything Aboli. And I do appreciate you helping me pack and make lists for everything but as of now I just

want to be with you for a little more time."
Saying that he kissed my forehead. We cuddled and appreciated each other's presence for one last time.

By six in the evening, the cab had arrived we were loading Aaroha's luggage in the car. His mom was standing beside us. Aaroha looked at her moist eyes. It was hard for her to leave the house which held the most amazing memories of her lifetime. She came to me and gave me a warm hug.
"Promise me you'll look after this house every once in a while. Water all the plants and maintain the garden. And don't let a single particle of dust settle on my Sarang's instruments." She said
"I promise you, aunty. I'll take care of your home." I assured her.
She sat in the cab to give Aaroha and me a few lone minutes.

I was already sobbing. I didn't want to let him go but I had to. I had spent every second of my day with him for the last 8 months. How was I supposed to live with this void? The void of his absence.
"Aaroha, promise me we are forever," I said
"Honey, yes we are and always will be," Aaroha said gently wiping off my tears with his thumb.
"Don't fall sick and take care of aunty. FaceTime me thrice a day. Text me after every

four hours. I want to be updated on each and everything about you and aunty and your college and London. Don't go alone to the places we have planned to visit together. I'm sorry I'm being a stupid annoying girlfriend but..."

Before I could finish Aaroha kissed me. He had teared up as well. Our heads pressed against each other, and we smiled with tears in our eyes. And said, "Let infinite love be always and forever in our hearts."

Aaroha hugged me and made his way towards the cab. He waved goodbye until the turning finally made me disappear from the rearview mirror. I got back home, went to the balcony, lit up a cigarette, and looked up at the sky waiting for the lights of the plane to sparkle up the moonless night. When it happened, I took my whiteboard and wrote, "Goodbye Aaroha, see you in six months."

To Be Continued...